ALICE & GERT

Written by
HELAINE BECKER

Illustrated by
DENA SEIFERLING

OWLKIDS BOOKS

IN A LUSH GREEN MEADOW,
there once lived an ant, Alice,
and a grasshopper, Gert.

Every morning when Gert woke up, she'd see Alice
at work, ferrying bits of grain and seeds to her nest.

One dewy morning, Gert called out,
"Hello, Alice! Isn't it a lovely summer day?"

Alice grunted under her heavy load.
"It may be nice now, but winter's on its way."

Gert laughed. "Winter is YEARS away.
Why don't you relax and enjoy this fine weather?"

"There'll be plenty of time to relax come January,"
said Alice.

The next morning, as Alice lugged a particularly heavy nut to her nest, she heard singing.

It's summer, it's summer, enjoy this fine day!
Life is for living, not toiling away!
Put down your load, and come laugh with me.
We'll play "Ring-a-Rosie" and sip flower tea.

It was Gert.

Alice stopped. "Did you write that song for me?"

"Yes," Gert said. "I hate to see you work so hard."

"But winter is coming! We must get ready!"

Gert leaned back on her
branch and picked up a soft green maple key.
"Who can think about winter on such a nice day?"

Alice harrumphed. But as she returned to work,
she found herself humming Gert's tune.

One golden morning, Gert leaped in front of Alice and shouted, "Ahoy, Alice!"

Alice paused in her work. "What's that?"

"My pirate hat. I made one for you, too. I will delight you today with a reading of *The Adventures of Long Green Gert: A Play in Three Dastardly Acts.*"

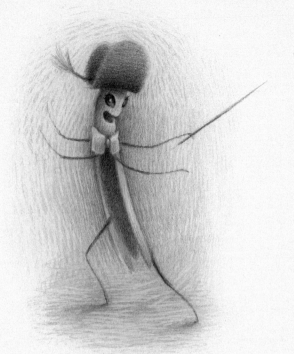

"Argh, you pusillanimous pillock, prepare to feel my wrath!"

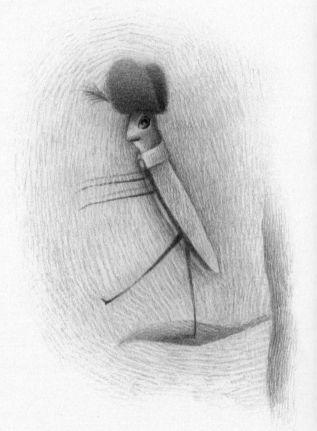

"Walk the plank!"

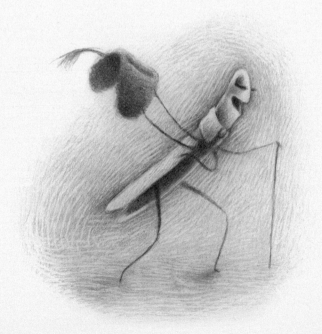

"Yo ho ho!"

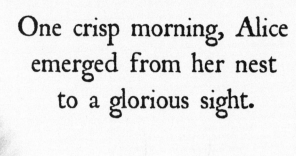

One crisp morning, Alice
emerged from her nest
to a glorious sight.

She barely felt the weight of her
labors that whole long day.

Until ...

One red leaf fluttered to the ground.

Gert sighed. "Isn't that beautiful? I shall dance to it. *The Dance of the Dying Spark.*"

Alice gasped. "Where's your sense, Gert? When the red leaves fall, it means winter is coming!"

Gert began her dance, a sarabande so soulful it brought tears to Alice's eyes.

What would happen to the sweet, flighty grasshopper
when all the summer seeds were gone?

One sparkling morning, Gert woke to find her nest rimed with frost. She shivered. "Can it be winter already?"

The grasshopper munched on a dry maple key and noticed there were no more on her nest. She shivered again.

"Good morning, Gert!" called out Alice.

"N-n-n-not working today?" asked Gert.

"No," replied Alice. "Winter is here, and there are no more seeds to collect."

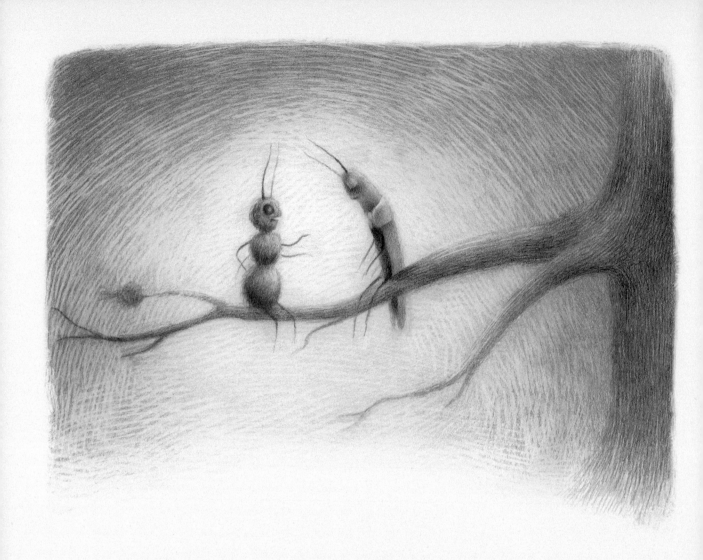

"What will I do?" moaned Gert. "I'll starve!"

"Perhaps you should have planned better,"
said Alice. "Instead, you sang and danced
through the long hard days of summer."

Gert hung her head.

"But," Alice continued, "your work lightened my load, and now it's time for me to repay your kindness. I've collected enough food to last the winter…"

"…for both of us."

In memory of
Alice B. Toklas, Gertrude
Stein, and Sheila Barry.
Great ladies all.
—H.B.

For my parents,
who raised me to value
creativity, hard work,
and kindness.
—D.S.

Owlkids Books acknowledges the financial support of the Canada Council for the Arts, the Ontario Arts Council, the Government of Canada through the Canada Book Fund (CBF) and the Government of Ontario through the Ontario Creates Book Initiative for our publishing activities.

Published in Canada by Owlkids Books Inc., 1 Eglinton Avenue East, Toronto, ON M4P 3A1
Published in the US by Owlkids Books Inc., 1700 Fourth Street, Berkeley, CA 94710

Library of Congress Control Number: 2019955615

Library and Archives Canada Cataloguing in Publication

Title: Alice & Gert / written by Helaine Becker ; illustrated by Dena Seiferling.
Other titles: Alice and Gert
Names: Becker, Helaine, author. | Seiferling, Dena, illustrator.
Identifiers: Canadiana 20190214570 | ISBN 9781771473583 (hardcover)
Classification: LCC PS8553.E295532 A7 2020 | DDC jC813/.6—dc23

Edited by Karen Li and Katherine Dearlove | Designed by Alisa Baldwin

Manufactured in Shenzhen, Guangdong, China, in February 2020, by WKT Co. Ltd.
Job #19CB2596

A   B   C   D   E   F

ONTARIO ARTS COUNCIL
CONSEIL DES ARTS DE L'ONTARIO
an Ontario government agency
un organisme du gouvernement de l'Ontario

Canada Council   Conseil des Arts
for the Arts   du Canada

Canadä

Publisher of Chirp, Chickadee and OWL
www.owlkidsbooks.com | Owlkids Books is a division of   bayard canada